Mom and Dad Don't Live Together Anymore

Story by Kathy Stinson
Art by Vian Oelofsen

annick press
toronto + new york + vancouver

j Sti

© 1984, 2007 Kathy Stinson (text)
© 2007 Vian Oelofsen (illustrations)
Design: Sheryl Shapiro

Annick Press Ltd.

We acknowledge the support of the Canada Council for the Arts, the Ontario Arts Council, and the Government of Canada through the Book Publishing Industry Development Program (BPIDP) for our publishing activities.

Cataloging in Publication

Stinson, Kathy
      Mom and Dad don't live together anymore / story by Kathy Stinson ; art by Vian Oelofsen.

ISBN 978-1-55451-094-8 (bound)
ISBN 978-1-55451-093-1 (pbk.)

    1. Divorce—Juvenile fiction.   2. Children of divorced parents—Juvenile fiction.

I. Oelofsen, Vian, 1974-   II. Title.

PS8587.T56M65 2007   jC813'.54   C2007-902354-1

The text was typeset in Billy Light.

Distributed in Canada by:
Firefly Books Ltd.
66 Leek Crescent
Richmond Hill, ON
L4B 1H1

Published in the U.S.A. by:
Annick Press (U.S.) Ltd.
Distributed in the U.S.A. by:
Firefly Books (U.S.) Inc.
P.O. Box 1338
Ellicott Station
Buffalo, NY 14205

Printed and bound in China.

Visit us at: www.annickpress.com

To my children, Matthew and Kelly. —K.S.

For my goddaughter, Abigail Elizabeth. —V.O.

My mommy and daddy don't live together anymore.

I live with my mommy and my brother
in an apartment in the city.

We go to Daddy's house in the country on weekends.

I like it at Mommy's apartment.
I like riding the elevators.
I like dropping garbage down the chute.

I like it at Daddy's house too.
I like feeding the horses at the farm down the road.
I like playing with my old friends.

If I had a wishbone I would wish
for us to all live together again.

Mommy and Daddy say that will never happen.
But I still wish it sometimes.

Dad, I wish you lived in the apartment across
the hall so I could see you every day.

I wonder if Daddy wants to get married with Paula.

Mom, when I grow up, will I get married and then get apart?

Last summer we went camping with Daddy.

Mommy played soccer with us at the park.

I like to be with Mommy.
She puts clips in my hair.
She takes me to ballet class.

I like to be with Daddy.
He gives me rides on his shoulders.
He takes me to Nana's for dinner.

I wonder where we'll be on Christmas.

I hope Santa knows.

Mommy says I make her happy.

Daddy says I make him happy.

I wish I could make them happy together.

I wonder why Mommy and Daddy can't make each other happy.
They say they tried and they can't anymore.
That's why they're separated.

I love my mommy and my daddy.

My mommy and my daddy love me too.

Just not together.